The Gift of the Giggles

Words by
LINDY CREEHAN KRAVEC

Art by
GEORGE TITONIS

Design by
JOE KRAVEC

A Small Press Selection
from Independent Publishers Group

Text copyright © 2005
by Lindy Creehan Kravec

Illustrations copyright © 2005
by George Titonis

All rights reserved.
No part of this publication
may be reproduced in whole
or in part, or stored in a
retrieval system or
transmitted in any form
by any means electronic,
mechanical, photocopying,
recording, or otherwise
without first obtaining
written permission
from the publisher.

ISBN: 0-9765398-0-2
Printed in the U.S.A.

BELLABOOZLE BOOKS
inc.

For Isabella and Alexandra and the ones who will giggle later.

L ong ago and far away there was a quiet little kingdom of grown-ups.

It was a very nice kingdom, with no toys in the yard or fingerprints on the windows.

The grown-ups were busy.

Every morning they hurried off to work.

They walked their dogs and polished their cars.

The kingdom was very nice, but something was missing.

The grown-ups had parties. But they would just sit and talk.

They played games. But they never jumped around.

One day, the Princess noticed that life was far too boring in the kingdom.

Something had to be done.

We need a *baby* in this kingdom!

A *baby*?

Yes! A *baby*!

A baby will change everything.

And so a baby was delivered.

The minute she opened her bright eyes, the grown-ups all smiled.

When she clapped her little hands, the smiles grew bigger.

And when she spattered her baby cereal all over the royal kitchen, all the grown-ups gasped!

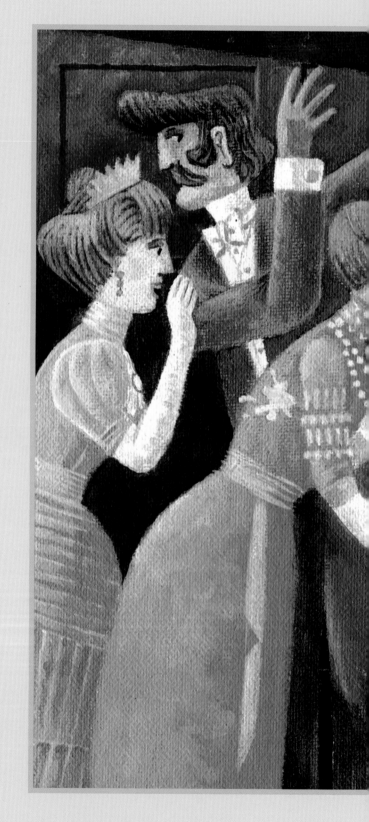

Then something amazing happened.

The grown-ups began to laugh.

At first it was a little titter… then it grew into a tee-hee… then a HA-HA… and a HO-HO-HO!

The baby began to shriek with delight, and the grown-ups shrieked with her.

Before you knew it, the whole kingdom was giggling.

They giggled all day and all night, and all through the next day.

They giggled so much that their faces hurt, and their tummies, too.

Finally, they were so exhausted, they fell asleep in one big pile of giggles.

When they awoke, they found all that giggling had made them hungry.

They ate and ate until their plates were clean. "Look," cried the Princess, "Every plate is a happy plate!"

"Goo-goo, Gaa-gaa!" agreed the baby.

"Splat!" went the last of the baby cereal.

From that day on, there were giggles everywhere. In fact, there was a Royal Decree that everyone in the kingdom must giggle at every meal.

Soon other babies were delivered to the kingdom. Every day at dinnertime, silly sounds spilled out of every home.

They rolled down the walkways and into the gardens.

The kingdom was a happy place because one little baby brought the gift of laughter to everyone.

The End

(Of quiet)

And The Beginning

(Of wonderful things)